P9-CEY-396

This book was a
gift to the
~~Sol Feinstone~~
~~Elementary School~~
~~Library to honor~~
~~the birthday of~~

DISCARDED

DISCARDED

Digby and Kate and the Beautiful Day

Digby

and the

Dutton Children's Books

New York

and Kate
Beautiful Day

DISCARDED

Barbara Baker

pictures by

Marsha Winborn

KATE

Digby did This

For Judy Gershowitz
B.A.B.

For Dee and Susan!
M.W.

Text copyright © 1998 by Barbara A. Baker
Illustrations copyright © 1998 by Marsha Winborn
All rights reserved.
CIP Data is available.
Published in the United States 1998 by Dutton Children's Books,
a member of Penguin Putnam Inc.
375 Hudson Street, New York, New York 10014
Printed in Hong Kong
First Edition
2 4 6 8 10 9 7 5 3 1
ISBN 0-525-45855-7

CONTENTS

WARM AND TASTY

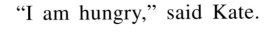

"I am hungry," said Kate.

"I want something to eat."

"What do you want?" said Digby.

"I want something warm and tasty,"

said Kate.

"I want something that is just right."

Kate went over to

a little hole in the wall.

"Oh, no," said Digby.

"Oh, yes," said Kate.

She sat down.

"Come out, come out, little mouse,"

she said.

But the mouse did not come out.

8

Digby sat down beside Kate.

"Go away, Digby," she said.

"You are too noisy.

The mouse will never come out."

So Digby went away.

Kate sat and sat.

Then she sat some more.

But the mouse did not come out.

Kate was getting very hungry.

"I will never have something

warm and tasty to eat," she said.

"I will not have anything at all."

Just then Kate smelled something.

It smelled wonderful.

Kate got up.

She went into the kitchen.

Digby was taking a pan

out of the oven.

"Pizza!" cried Kate.

"I love pizza."

Digby and Kate sat

at the kitchen table.

They ate pizza.

It was warm.

It was tasty.

It was just right.

CHECKERS

"Do you want to play checkers?"

said Kate.

"Okay," said Digby.

Kate set up the checkers.

"I go first," she said.

"Why?" said Digby.

"Cats before dogs," said Kate.

"That is the rule."

Kate moved a checker one space.

Digby moved a checker one space.

Kate moved a checker two spaces.

Then she jumped over Digby's checker.

"Hey!" said Digby.

"You can't do that."

"Yes I can," said Kate.

"It is my game."

"Maybe we should read the rules first,"

said Digby.

"No," said Kate.

"I know how to play.

Now it is your turn, Digby.

Go ahead."

Digby moved a checker.

"Aha!" he said.

"I am going to get you."

"No, you will not," said Kate.

She moved her checker sideways.

"Kate!" cried Digby.

"You cannot move sideways.

It is against the rules."

18

"But I *had* to," said Kate.

"You were going to jump me."

Digby groaned.

"Are you sure you know how

to play this game?" he said.

Kate put the checker back.

She moved a different one.

"Hooray!" said Digby.

"Now I have a double jump."

"That's not fair," cried Kate.

"You tricked me."

"I did not," said Digby.

Kate moved another checker.

"I am going to win this game," she said.

Digby jumped Kate's checker.

"King me," he said.

"No," said Kate.

"Why not?" said Digby.

"Because it is *my* game," said Kate.

"That is the rule."

Digby groaned again.

A fly buzzed into the room.

It flew around Digby.

It flew around Kate.

Kate tried to hit the fly.

She hit the checker game instead.

Checkers flew into the air.

"Oh, dear," said Kate.

"Now we will have to start

all over again."

"Yes," said Digby.

"But this time we will go to *my* house.

We will use *my* game."

"Why?" said Kate.

"Because," said Digby.

"That is *my* rule."

THE CAMERA

Digby had a new camera.

He wanted to take pictures

of everything.

He saw a bug.

Click.

He took a picture.

He saw a tree.

Click.

He took a picture.

Digby took many pictures.

He took pictures of little things.

He took pictures of big things.

28

"This is fun," he said.

"It is not fun for me," said Kate.

"I want you to stop."

"Just one more," said Digby.

"Then I will let *you*

have a turn."

Click.

He took a picture of a flower.

Then Digby gave the camera to Kate.

"Thank you, Digby," said Kate.

She put the camera in her pocket.

"Why did you do that?" said Digby.

"Because," said Kate, "it is my turn."

"But I do not want to take pictures.

I want to *chase* bugs.

I want to *climb* trees.

I want to *smell* flowers."

And that is just what she did.

MARKERS

32

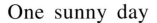

One sunny day

Digby came to Kate's house.

"Let's go for a walk," he said.

"Not now," said Kate.

"Come see what I have.

I have some new markers."

33

She took the markers

out of the box.

"I have red and blue and yellow

and orange and green and purple

and black and brown."

"That's nice," said Digby.

"Now, let's go for a walk."

"Sit down, Digby," said Kate.

"I am going to draw a picture of you."

Digby sat down.

Kate started to draw.

"This is going to be

a wonderful picture," she said.

"It is going to be perfect."

"But I want to go for a walk,"

said Digby.

"Hold still," said Kate. "Don't move."

36

Digby was still.

Kate worked and worked

and worked and worked.

She used every marker.

She used red and blue and yellow

and orange and green and purple

and black and brown.

She worked for a long, long time.

Digby sneezed.

"Hold still," said Kate.

Digby wiggled.

"Don't move," said Kate.

Digby groaned.

"I am almost finished," said Kate.

Finally she was done.

"Look," she said. "It is perfect."

"Good," said Digby.

"Now, can we go for a walk?"

"Not yet," said Kate.

"First I want *you*

to make a picture of *me.*"

Digby looked at the markers.

He looked at the sun

outside Kate's window.

Then he took his camera

out of his pocket.

Click.

He was done.

"Perfect," said Digby.

"Now we can go

for a good, long walk."

THE WALK

It was a beautiful sunny day.

Then the sun went behind

a big dark cloud.

"Come back, sun," called Digby.

"We want to go for a walk."

But the sun did not come back.

It began to rain.

"Oh, no!" said Digby.

"Now we cannot go for a walk.

We cannot feel the sun on our heads.

We cannot run in the grass.

We cannot pick flowers."

"Don't be sad," said Kate.

"I have an idea."

She opened her door.

She went outside.

"Come on, Digby," she said.

"Let's go."

Kate and Digby went for a long, wet walk.

They felt the raindrops on their heads.

They ran through mud puddles.

They picked some very wet flowers.

Then they went home.

"That was fun," said Digby.

Outside it was still raining.

But Digby and Kate didn't mind.

Kate put the flowers in a glass.

Then she made some

cocoa and cinnamon toast.

Digby and Kate drank cocoa

and ate cinnamon toast.

They watched the rain

outside the window.

It was a beautiful rainy day.

E
B

Baker, Barbara.

Digby and Kate and
the beautiful day.

$13.99

75359

DISCARDED

DATE			

SOL FEINSTONE ELEM. SCHOOL
LIBRARY
EAGLE ROAD, BOX 116
NEWTOWN, PA   18940
10/22/1998 $13.99

BAKER & TAYLOR